DRAGLINS

For Tyler, with love
x VF

For Pearl, with love
CF

ORCHARD BOOKS
338 Euston Road, London NW1 3BH
Orchard Books Australia
Level 17/207, Kent Street, Sydney, NSW 2000
First published in Great Britain in 2007
First paperback publication 2008
Text © copyright Vivian French 2007
Illustrations © copyright Chris Fisher 2007
The rights of Vivian French and Chris Fisher to be
identified as the author and illustrator of this work
have been asserted by them in accordance with
the Copyright, Designs and Patents Act, 1988.

A CIP catalogue record for this book is
available from the British Library.

ISBN 978 1 84362 698 5 (hardback)
ISBN 978 1 84362 707 4 (paperback)

1 3 5 7 9 10 8 6 4 2 (hardback)
1 3 5 7 9 10 8 6 4 2 (paperback)
Printed in Great Britain by
Antony Rowe Ltd, Chippenham, Wiltshire
Orchard Books is a division of Hachette Children's Books,
an Hachette Livre UK company.
www.orchardbooks.co.uk

DRAGLINS AND THE FLOOD!

VIVIAN FRENCH   CHRIS FISHER

ORCHARD BOOKS

CHAPTER ONE

"**I**s everybody neat and tidy?" Aunt Plum asked. "And have you all got your boots on? And your waterproofs buttoned up? It's POURING with rain outside."

"Yes, Aunt Plum," Dora said politely. Danny nodded. Dennis, who was still eating toast, made a gulping noise. Daffodil grunted.

Uncle Damson stepped forward, and cleared his throat. "Ahem. Now, listen carefully! You are going to meet a VERY important old draglin! Great Grandmother Attica is my grandmother, and your – er – "

"Great Grandmother!" Daffodil said brightly.

"Erm – exactly, Daffodil. I'm glad to see you're paying attention." Uncle Damson puffed out his chest, and began again. "You must be on your VERY best behaviour. Great Grandmother Attica has never met you before, and I would like – " Uncle Damson stared hard at Daffodil and Dennis – "I would like her to think that Aunt Plum and I have brought you up to be good, polite little draglins. Do you think you could manage that, just for one day?"

There were faint murmurings from Dennis, Danny and Daffodil, and a clearer "Yes, Uncle Damson!" from Dora.

"Good. And one last thing – be sure to give her my very best wishes." Uncle Damson sat down again, and helped himself to more acorn bread. "Plum, have you given them a gift to take?"

Aunt Plum nodded. "I've packed up a bag of dried berries," she said, and then glanced out of the window. "But

I'm still not sure they should go. It's raining so hard."

At the other end of the breakfast table Uncle Plant rustled his Weekly Draglin.

"Don't fuss, Plum," he growled. "A spot more rain won't stop them. Never has before, if the mud in the hallway's anything to judge by."

"Actually, we don't mind not going," Danny said. "There's lots of things we can do here."

"That's what I'm afraid of." Uncle Puddle joined Aunt Plum at the window. "Weather doesn't look any worse than usual. Send them off, Plum. They've been under our feet for days. Can't think why they need school holidays – all they do is make a mess everywhere."

"That's very true," Uncle Damson agreed. "Besides, it's all arranged. Rick and Rigger are meeting our four in the Underground, and taking them to the edge of the Great Wetness. They'll row them over to Brid Island, and take them to Grandmother Attica's house. They'll be perfectly safe, and it'll keep them out of trouble."

Aunt Plum sighed. "You'd better be off, then, children. But make sure you do EXACTLY what Rick tells you, and DO be polite to your great grandmother!" She picked up the bag of berries, and handed it to Danny. "Don't lose it," she warned. Then she turned to Dora. "DO make sure you all keep nice and clean, dear. Daffodil—"

"Goodbye, Aunt Plum!" Daffodil swung her backpack onto her shoulder and zoomed out of the kitchen before Aunt Plum could say anything else.

"Oi! Wait for me!" Dennis said, and rushed after her. Danny and Dora hurried behind, Dora pausing only to drop a kiss on the top of her little cousin Pip's head.

"Yuck." Pip rubbed at the kiss with one hand, and waved with the other. "Bye bye!"

CHAPTER TWO

"Phew!" Dennis said as they splashed out from Under Shed, across the boggy grass, and into the Underground. "And now for an adventure!"

Dora looked anxious. "But we're going to see our great grandmother, aren't we?"

Dennis began to swagger. "Maybe, but you know what Rick's like. Adventures just happen wherever he goes. Same as me."

"And me," Daffodil said.

"But we don't have to have adventures," Dora objected. "We could have a lovely peaceful day out instead."

"BORING!" Daffodil and Dennis shouted together.

"It'll be OK, Dor," Danny said soothingly. "Besides, look what you did last time we met Rick and Rigger. You scared off a chat."

Dora shuddered. "But I never want to do that again."

"LOOK!" Daffodil suddenly stopped dead, and Dennis, Dora and Danny piled into her.

"OW!" Dennis had bumped his head. "What's up, Daffy?"

Daffodil pointed at the ground in front of her. "It's a message!" she said excitedly.

"YEAH! It's a CLUE!" Dennis looked at the arrow made of sticks. "Told you we were going to have an adventure!"

"How do we know it's from Rick and Rigger?" Danny asked.

"Who else would it be from? Come on – down this way!" And Dennis hurtled off down a side tunnel, in the direction of the pointing arrow.

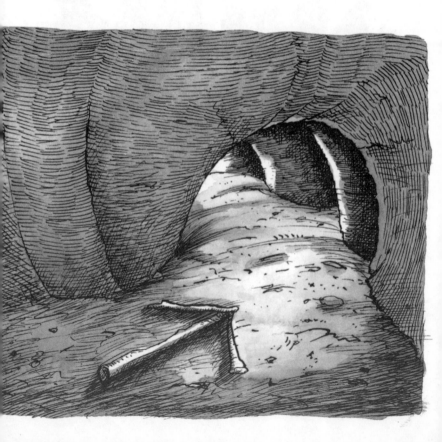

The tunnel was narrower than the draglins were used to, and twistier. Even Dora was reassured, however, because every time there was a doubtful bend the way was marked. All the same, she hoped it wouldn't be too long before she saw her cousins in person.

"Ooops!" Dennis stopped. Something had disturbed the next arrow, and bits of stick were scattered over the ground. It was impossible to tell which way it had pointed, and they were standing at a crossroads.

"We could try each way in turn until we see another arrow," Danny suggested.

"I think we should take a tunnel each," Daffodil said. "It'd be quicker."

Dora was staring at the bits of stick. "What do you think muddled them up?" she asked nervously. "It might be something fierce!"

Dennis flung himself down on the ground. "I can't see any footprints," he reported. "But it must have gone by quite recently. I bet Rick left the arrows here this morning."

Daffodil's eyes lit up. "Ooooh! Maybe it's a wild mowser with long sharp teeth!"

"Or a simply ginormous spiddle with eight hairy legs," Dennis said.

"Or it might be just another draglin," Danny offered. "What do you think, Dor?"

Dora didn't answer. She was listening, her head on one side. "I can hear something!" she whispered.

There was silence as all four draglins strained their ears.

"I think it's down that way," Danny said at last. "Should we go and see?"

"Yes." Dora sounded surprisingly firm. "It's a sort of squeaking. I think it's hurt." And she was the first to set off in the direction of the noise.

CHAPTER THREE

The duckling was crouched against the tunnel wall, covered in dust and looking thoroughly miserable. It was nibbling at half a stick, but it dropped it when the draglins came hurrying towards it.

"OH!" Dora said. "You poor poor thing!"

The duckling tried to flap its dirty wings, and took a step backwards.

"Shhhh," Dora said soothingly. "We won't hurt you!" And she gently stroked its head.

"How do you think it got in here?" Danny asked.

"Maybe something chased it in," Dennis said. "A chat, or a dawg. Maybe it came from the Great Wetness."

Daffodil was looking at the duckling thoughtfully. "We could keep it and tame it," she suggested. "Then when it's bigger we could ride on it! In fact – " Daffodil began to hop up and down in excitement – "we could travel all over the Great Wetness and explore!"

"Peep," said the duckling anxiously. "Peep!"

"Honestly, Daffy," Danny said. "You're completely mad! Where on earth would we keep a great big duckle? Aunt Plum would have a fit!"

Dennis had wandered off. "Hey!" he called back. "I've found another arrow! We're in the right tunnel!"

"Good." Dora put her arm round the duckling's neck. "Come on, little ducklet. We'll take you to the Great Wetness, and then you'll be fine."

Persuading the duckling to go with

them was much easier said than done. It was determined to stay where it was, and resisted all Dora's encouraging noises.

"We're going to be really late if we don't get moving," Dennis said at last.

"And the great-grandmother will be cross!" Daffodil added.

"But we can't leave it!" Dora said, tears in her eyes. "It'll starve! Look how skinny it is!"

Danny fished in the bag Aunt Plum had given him. "Here, duckie duckie!" he said, and held out a berry.

The duckling moved so fast that all three draglins jumped, and Danny hastily dropped the berry. It was gone in a second.

"WOW!" Danny said. "It is hungry!"

The duckling looked hopefully at the basket. "Peep!" it said. "Peep?"

Danny gave it another berry, then walked away. At once the duckling pattered

after him, peeping softly.

"Well done, Danny," Dennis said.

"And look! There's another arrow!" Daffodil beamed. "And it's getting lighter...the end of the tunnel can't be far away."

Daffodil was right. Two more arrows, and three berries for the duckling, and they were at the Underground exit. Outside they could see rough grass, bent down by rain, and beyond the grass was a low brick wall.

"What do we do now?" Danny asked. "I can't see any more arrows, and I can't see Rick or Rigger either."

"And it's still pouring," Dora said. "Aunt Plum was right."

The duckling gave a loud "PEEP!" and paddled outside. It shook its feathers, and began to preen itself.

"Isn't it SWEET?" Dora breathed.

"QUACK!"

The duckling froze.

"QUACK QUACK QUACK!"

The duckling ran into the grass, and wriggled its way through to the wall. With a great deal of scrambling and flapping it managed to reach the top, and for a second it balanced there precariously.

There was one more quack, then a SPLASH! as the duckling disappeared.

"WOW! Did you hear that?" Dennis asked. "That's WATER! We must be right beside the Great Wetness – quick! Let's go and see!" And forgetting all Uncle Damson and Aunt Plum's careful training, he dashed out of the Underground. Daffodil tore after him.

Danny and Dora looked at each other. "We'd better follow them," Danny said. "If there's anything dangerous around we'd have heard it by now...wouldn't we?"

Dora nodded, and the two more cautious draglins tiptoed towards the wall.

CHAPTER FOUR

"It's HUGE!" Even Daffodil was astonished by the size of the lake.

Dora was staring at it in horror. The wind and the rain were ruffling the surface of the water into choppy little waves, and the thought of rowing out on it made her sick with terror.

Beside her, Danny pulled the hood of his waterproof tighter over his ears. "I can't see Brid Island!" he said. "Can you, Dennis?"

Dennis was striding about the top of the wall like a captain on board his ship. "We'll have a rough voyage," he announced. "I wouldn't be surprised if we were…"

He didn't finish his sentence. A rope soared into the air from below, circled round him, and neatly pinned his arms to his sides.

"YIKES!" Dennis yelled as he was

whisked off the wall to a muddy landing at the water's edge. "GERROFFF!" And he struggled into a sitting position, pulling at the rope to free himself.

"That'll teach you to go hopping up and down where anyone can catch you." Rick was standing over Dennis, the end of the rope in his hand. "You're dead lucky it's raining, and all the Human Beanies are indoors. Isn't that right, Rigger?"

There was a rumbling sound, and Dennis saw Rigger, Rick's twin brother, leaning against the wall.

"Rigger says you're daft," Rick interpreted.

Dennis looked at his teenage cousins, trying to make up his mind if he was impressed or angry. Daffodil made up his mind for him as she jumped down beside him, glowing with enthusiasm.

"That was so COOL, Rick!" she gasped. "Can you show me how to do that?"

"And me!" Dennis struggled to his feet, mud clinging to his clothes.

"Me too!" Danny appeared, followed by Dora. "It was BRILLIANT!"

Rigger looked at Dora, and she smiled unwillingly. "It was VERY clever," she admitted, "but it did give me a terrible fright."

"Was meant to," Rick said. "You're getting careless. Most Beanies aren't allowed round here – it's a brid sanctuary – but sometimes the keepers come stomping about. And I've seen chats here too, from time to time. You must ALWAYS keep a look out!"

Dennis and Daffodil shifted uncomfortably, and Dennis said, "Sorry."

Rigger rumbled again.

"He says he's pleased to see you, even if you are daft," Rick told them. "Are you ready for a boat ride?"

Dora was looking round. "Have you seen a ducklet?" she asked. "We were taking care of it, but it heard its mother calling and ran

30

off. I wanted to make sure it was safe."

Rigger grinned. "Quack," he said, and it was such a perfect duck noise Dora couldn't help laughing.

"It was YOU!" she said.

"Quack." Rigger pointed. Dora and the others moved nearer the water, and saw, hidden amongst the reeds, a neat little rowing boat. The duckling was nestled close beside it, but when it saw Danny it gave a cheerful "Peep!"

"We'd better take it with us," Rick said. "If we leave it here some chat'll have it for breakfast. It'll be quite safe on Brid Island. There aren't any chats there. Nor dawgs. Nor Beanies. That's right, isn't it, Rigger? It's the safest place in the world."

"Erm...where is Brid Island?" Dora asked, trying her best not to sound anxious. "Is it very far?"

"We don't care how far away it is, do we, Dennis?" Daffodil boasted. "And I don't mind rowing the boat, either."

Rick gave her a sideways look. "Have you ever rowed before?"

"No, but I can do it," Daffodil told him. "Aunt Plum's shown me pictures. LOADS of pictures."

Rigger's rumble and Rick's yelp were so loud that the duckling flapped its wings in agitation. Daffodil, furious at being laughed at, took a flying leap into the boat, yelling, "I CAN! I'll SHOW you!"

The boat rocked wildly on the water. Daffodil wobbled, staggered, clutched at the air…

…and fell in.

33

CHAPTER FIVE

I t took longer than it should have done to rescue Daffodil because Rick and Rigger were laughing too much to concentrate. By the time she was back on the bank she felt ashamed of herself, and was wondering if she could pretend she'd fallen in on purpose, as a joke. Deciding no one would believe her, she wiped a piece of weed off her ear, and grinned feebly. Dora, clucking with anxiety, pulled a dry sweater from her backpack and wrapped it round Daffodil's shivering shoulders.

"We ought to go home," she said. "Daffy'll catch a horrible cold."

Daffodil straightened herself. "No I won't," she snapped. "I'm not that much wetter than I was before. I want to go in the boat. AND I want to see the great-grandmother person."

"Ho!" Rick winked at Dora. "She'll like seeing you too. Won't she, Rigger?"

Rigger smiled, and nodded.

"But we CAN'T! Dennis is covered in mud, and Daffodil's dripping wet, and the ducklet's been eating the berries." Dora wrung her hands in distress. "Uncle Damson made us PROMISE we'd be clean and tidy, and not let him and Aunt Plum down."

Rigger patted Dora's arm, and rumbled an encouraging rumble. At once Dora looked more cheerful, and when Rick held out his hand she let him help her into the boat without a fuss.

"What did Rigger say?" Danny wanted to know.

"He says Great Gran won't care if we're clean or dirty." Dora giggled. "He says she lives like a brid, in a tree."

"REALLY?" Danny scrambled into the boat, and sat beside her. "Can't wait to meet her!" He rubbed his nose thoughtfully. "Does Uncle Damson know?"

"Shouldn't think so," Rick said as he showed Dennis and Daffodil where to sit. "They haven't met for years and years and years. Greatest Gran thinks he's...um... a bit pompous."

Dennis and Daffodil chortled, and Danny grinned. Dora, always loyal, tried to explain. "He doesn't really mean to be," she said. "It's just...it's just the way he says things."

"It's OK, Dora," Rick said as he picked up an oar. "We know what he's like. Don't we, Rigger?" And he and Rigger began to row with long sweeping strokes of their oars. The duckling paddled after them, encouraged by Rigger's quacks.

Although it was still raining, the wind had dropped. The boat sped across the water, and before long the four little draglins saw an island not far ahead. It was so low lying that it was difficult to see from the shore; even the branches of the straggling bushes drooped down into the water, and there was only one stunted tree.

"Water level's much too high," Rick said. "It's all this rain we've been having. The landing stage is underwater already."

"So how will we get out?" Dennis asked.

"We'll have to paddle," Rick told him.

As Rick brought the boat round, Rigger shipped his oar and stood up, the mooring rope in his hand. With practised ease he leapt out, pulling the boat behind him as he waded towards the island. At once Dennis leapt after him.

"Can I tie the boat up? Please?" he begged.

Rigger nodded, and handed Dennis the rope. Dennis grinned at Daffodil, and tied the rope to a twisted root with several large knots.

"Water's even higher than it was yesterday." Rick shook his head. "If this rain goes on, the whole island'll be underwater."

"Will we have to rescue Great Grandmother?" Daffodil hopped out and paddled to land. Even when she was out of the water the ground was sodden. Dora, splashing after Daffodil, had the uncomfortable feeling that the whole island might dissolve under her feet. Dennis and Danny, squelching happily, had no such worries.

"What a place!" Dennis said as he looked round. "Hey! I can see loads and LOADS of duckles! And – " his eyes opened very wide – "WHAT ON EARTH'S THAT?"

Rick turned to see what Dennis was looking at. "Oh," he said, "that's Great Grandmother Attica."

CHAPTER SIX

Dora had imagined that a great grandmother would be large and fierce. In fact, Great Grandmother Attica was tiny, much smaller than Dora. She was wearing a dress made of feathers, and was walking on stilts. From a distance she looked exactly like a bird.

"Hi, Greatest," Rick said as she moved swiftly towards them. "You've not met this lot. Dennis, Danny, Dora and Daffodil."

"Welcome, my dears." Great Grandmother's voice was shrill, like the whistle of a sea bird. "Welcome."

Dora stepped forward, and made her great grandmother an awkward curtsey. "How do you do?" she said politely. "If you please, we've brought you some berries." She elbowed Danny, and he pulled the half empty bag out of his jacket pocket.

"Berries?" Great Grandmother's eyes twinkled. "Got plenty of my own, thank you."

Danny silently put the berries back in his pocket.

"And," Dora struggled on, "Uncle Damson sends his very best wishes."

"Glad to hear it. Now, follow me! Soup's waiting." And Great Grandmother turned, and strode off towards the willow. As her great grandchildren waded after her the rain stopped, and a watery sun came out from behind the clouds.

"Hey!" Rick said. "Look at that! About time too, or the whole of Brid Island would be underwater."

"What would happen then?" Dennis wanted to know.

Rick shrugged. "It's happened before. When the rain stops, the water level goes down and the island reappears again."

"But what does Great Grandmother do?" Danny asked.

"Sits and waits," Rick said. "And the brids keep an eye on her, don't they, Rigger? Look – here we are. Take your boots off before you come in."

Dennis, Dora, Danny and Daffodil stared. They could see no sign of a house. In front of them was the stunted willow, its gnarled trunk twisted and bent and covered in moss. On either side was nothing but mud, more mud, and wet grass.

Rigger looked at their blank faces, and rumbled at Dora. She gave a gasp, and looked up into the branches. Not far above her head was a nest, and two branches higher was another one. From below they looked like piles of sticks.

"I'm not very good at climbing trees in my boots," Dora began, but Rigger stopped her by tapping on the tree trunk. A neat front door, impossible to see when it was closed, swung wide open. Inside was a small room, empty except for Great Grandmother's stilts, a row of coat hooks with a fishing rod balanced on top, and a good deal of mud. A spiral staircase led invitingly upwards.

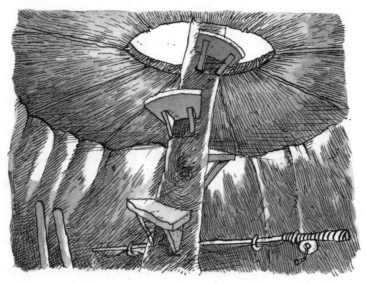

"WOW!" Dennis breathed. "That's fantastic!"

"Peep!" As the draglins pulled off their boots and hung up their waterproofs, the duckling appeared in the doorway. It looked hopefully at Danny. "Peep?"

"Here you are, little thing," Danny said, and tossed a couple of dried berries over its head onto the grass. As the duckling hurried to find them, Rick gently shut the door.

"She'd never manage the stairs," he said. "Come on up."

Daffodil rushed forward. "We're coming!"

47

CHAPTER SEVEN

The staircase took them up and up, and into a much larger room where a wicker bench circled the walls. Above the bench were rows of shelves piled high with crockery, moss, clothes, bunches of herbs, bits of string, bags of nuts – everything an ancient draglin might ever need. In the middle of the floor a glowing fire was burning in a metal stove, and Great Grandmother was bent over it stirring something in a battered saucepan. There was a warm spicy smell in the air that made the little draglins realise just how hungry they were.

"Dandelion and cob nut, flavoured with nasturtium," said Great Grandmother. "Daffodil, get the bowls from the shelf. Dennis, you'll find bread by the door. Rigger, spoons."

The draglins scurried about doing as they were told. In no time at all they were sitting on the bench sipping at steaming bowls of soup.

"This is DELICIOUS," Dora said. "Thank—"

"R R R R R R R R R R M M M M ! RRRRRRRRRRRRRRMMMMM!"

The room began to tremble, and Dora

stopped mid-sentence. Rick and Rigger sprang to their feet, and leapt to the shaking shelves where plates, jugs and jars were dancing up and down.

"Bloomin' Beanies!" Rigger said as he caught a teapot, but missed a falling saucepan. "Thought they'd stopped doing that!"

"What are they doing?" Daffodil shot forward just in time to save a basket of acorns.

"It's a boat with an engine," Rick told her as he juggled with several bags of herbs at once. "Dennis – open those shutters, and see what's happening!"

Dennis flew to the window, and flung the shutters wide. Standing on the wicker bench, he peered out.

"The boat's going past," he reported. "There's one Beanie driving, and another looking round." He leant out further. "Hey! The boat's leaving loads of waves behind. OH! Oh NO! They're coming this way..."

"That's just what I was afraid of," Rigger said grimly. "Keep your fingers crossed that they don't—"

WHOOOSH!

The waves flooded across Brid Island. For a moment Dennis could see no land at all, except for a few twigs sticking up to mark where the bushes grew. Only the willow tree rose above the swirling muddy water.

"WOW!" Dennis said, overawed. "WOW!"

"It'll go down again," Great Grandmother said calmly. "It always does."

Danny, Dora and Daffodil joined Dennis at the window. A flurry of ducks swam past, looking as if they were quite used to having no land. The duckling peeped cheerfully at them as it bobbed up and down under the shadow of the branches.

"But how will we get back to our boat?" Dora asked anxiously.

"Keep watching," Rick said, and even as he spoke the waters were beginning to go down. First one bush and then another reappeared, and at last the long low shape of Brid Island stretched out again below the willow.

Dennis climbed down from the bench. "The island's back again," he said.

There was a thoughtful rumble from Rigger, and he went to look out of the window. At once he let out a long whistle, and Rick hurried to see what he was looking at.

"Ah." Rick rubbed his head. "See what you mean, Rigger. Bit of a problem, that."

"What is it?" Daffodil pushed Rigger out of the way. "Where is it? Where's the problem?"

"No boat," Rick said.

"What?" Daffodil stared at him.

Rick shrugged. "Our boat. It's gone. Must have been washed away in the flood."

CHAPTER EIGHT

Dennis felt terrible. "I tied it up with my very best knots," he said for the twentieth time. "I really did."

Rick slapped him on the back. "No good fretting about it. If it's gone, it's gone. Isn't that right, Rigger?"

Rigger rumbled comfortingly.

"It'll turn up again in time," Rick went on. "It won't sink – that's for sure."

"We'll be OK here until you find it," Daffodil said, and she sat down and folded her arms. "We can learn to walk on stilts, and we can train the ducklet."

"Daffy!" Dora was staring at her in horror. "We can't stay here! What will Aunt Plum think? We've got to get home!"

"And what happens if the boat ends up on the other side of the Great Wetness?" Danny wanted to know.

Daffodil refused to be gloomy. "We can swim across."

Great Grandmother Attica let out a shrill scream of laughter. "I LIKE you," she told Daffodil.

Daffodil beamed. "I do have very VERY good ideas," she said.

"No you don't. That's why I like you. You have the most ridiculous ideas!" Great Grandmother laughed again. "No draglin could ever swim that far. We'll have to think of something else."

58

Danny was still peering out of the window. "Are those nests used?" he asked. "Do brids still nest in them?"

The old draglin looked at him, her eyes bright. "Those, young Danny, are my summer bedrooms. But I can see what you're thinking. You're obviously the one with the clever ideas."

Daffodil snorted loudly. "No, he's not! And what use is a nest? We need a boat!"

Dora sat up very straight. "But nests are made of twigs, and twigs are wood, and wood floats! Oh, Danny – that's a brilliant idea!"

Dennis was feeling left out, and it made him cross. "It's a stupid idea. How will we row it? We haven't any oars."

Dora jumped to her feet. "I know! The ducklet can tow it!"

"That has to be the WORST idea ever!" Daffodil cackled. "How on earth will you make it go the way you want it to?"

"It'll go round and round in circles until we're dizzy!" Dennis hooted. "It'll be a dizzy ducklet! And you'll be dizzy Dora!"

"No I won't, and neither will the ducklet." Dora frowned at him. "We can put a berry on the end of Great Grandmother's fishing line, and hold it in front of her."

There was a silence as everyone stared at Dora. She blushed, and looked at her feet. "I just thought...I'm sorry if it was a silly idea."

"It wasn't silly, my dear." Great Grandmother Attica smiled at her. "It was a very clever idea. And as soon as we're quite sure the Beanies aren't going to come back again we're going to try your idea out. Dennis, fetch me my fishing rod. Danny – where are those berries? Rick and Rigger, I want that nest off that branch and down on the ground. Daffodil, you can help them."

CHAPTER NINE

The hardest part was dragging the nest from under the tree to the water's edge.

It took all the draglins pushing and pulling together to get it there, and by the time it was floating every single one of them was covered in mud from head to foot.

The duckling pattered beside them. Every so often she gave Danny a meaningful look, and said, "Peep?" with her head on one side, and he would stop and throw her a berry. She was only too happy to let him slip a soft harness made from Great Grandmother's wool scraps over her head.

"Now, are you ready?" Great Grandmother asked as the six young draglins arranged themselves in the nest. "Rick and Rigger, make sure the little ones don't do anything foolish." She saw Daffodil's outraged face, and smiled. "And come and see me again soon. I haven't laughed so much for a long time! Now – be off with you!" And as Danny dangled the berry in front of the duckling, the nest began to move slowly away from the island.

"Goodbye!" Great Grandmother called. "Goodbye!"

"NOOOOOOOO! We can't! We can't go like this!" It was Dora. "QUICK! Turn back! We've got to turn back NOW!"

CHAPTER TEN

D anny, Dennis, Daffodil, Rick and Rigger looked at Dora in astonishment.

"Whatever's the matter, Dor?" Danny asked.

"It's the ducklet!" Dora wailed. "If it tows us across to the other side it'll get left there after we've gone home and it'll get eaten by a chat because Rick said it would and it'll be all my fault!" Dora stopped to take a breath. "Oh – I'm so horribly horribly SELFISH!" And she burst into tears.

Danny hesitated, and the duckling took the opportunity to gobble up the berry tied to the end of the fishing line. Rigger leant forward to pat Dora's hand, and the nest rocked alarmingly.

"SIT STILL!" Rick roared, and as they froze, the nest steadied itself. Rigger rumbled to himself, and Rick shook his head at Dora. "Don't you know Great Grandmother loves brids? Of course she's thought of that!"

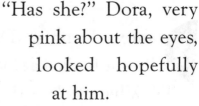

"Has she?" Dora, very pink about the eyes, looked hopefully at him.

"Quack," said Rigger softly. "Quack quack."

From the island behind them came an answering call. "Quack. Quack quack quack."

"PEEP!" The duckling flapped its little wings.

"OH!" Dora sighed with relief. "Great Grandmother can talk duckle too!"

"Who do you think taught Rigger?" Rick asked her. "Now, get another berry on that line, double quick."

*

The rest of the journey went peacefully. The duckling towed the nest like a small feathered machine, and as the draglins paddled their way to the shore, Danny rewarded her with a handful of berries.

"Don't give her too many or she'll not want to go home," Dennis warned him, but the moment the duckling heard the call from across the water she was off.

"She'll be happy with Great Grandmother," Rick said. "She'll get to know all the other duckles on the island, and before you know it she'll be a fully grown duckle herself."

"Can we come and see her sometimes?" Dora asked. "And Great Grandmother too."

"Of course you can." Rick grinned at her. "But wait until we've got the boat back. Easier that way, isn't it, Rigger?"

Rigger rumbled an enthusiastic agreement.

Danny squinted up at the evening sky. "We'd better be going home," he said. "Thanks for a great day out."

Daffodil, Dennis and Dora nodded. "It was FABULOUS!" Daffodil said.

"FANTASTIC!" said Dennis.

"BRILLIANT!" said Dora.

Rick and Rigger looked at the four mud-caked little draglins. "Well," Rick said, "if you think falling in the Great Wetness, getting flooded and covered in mud is a great day out, that's EASY. We'll do it again soon!" And he and Rigger watched, smiling, as Dennis, Daffodil, Danny and Dora climbed over the wall and squelched off to the Underground.

"What'll Aunt Plum and Uncle Damson say when they see them?" Rick wondered.

Rigger rumbled an answer.

"Quite right," Rick said. "Much better not to think about it..."

HAVE YOU
READ ALL THE
DRAGLINS BOOKS?

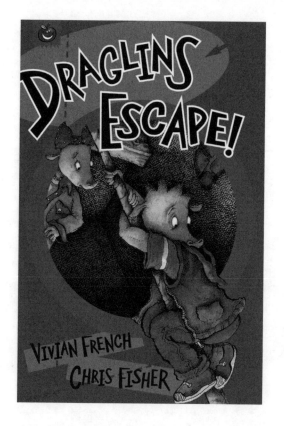

Daffodil, Dora, Dennis and Danny
can't believe they are moving to the great
Outdoors! How will they get down from
Under Roof? And will they get to see the
scary chats and dawgs they've
heard so much about?

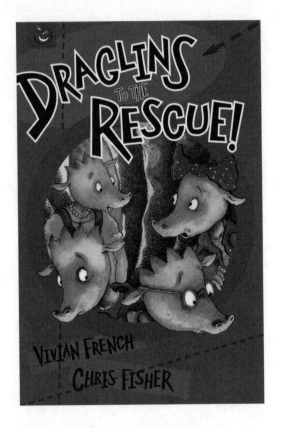

Daffodil, Dora, Dennis and Danny
have moved Outdoors, but their things are
trapped Under Roof! Dennis has a PLAN
to rescue them... But will the gigantic
Human Beanies get in the way?

Wowling has been heard near the draglins'
home in Under Shed! Daffodil, Dora, Dennis
and Danny come face to face with a scary chat
for the first time ever – are four little
draglins a match for terrible
teeth and sharp claws?

What will draglin school in the great
Outdoors be like? Daffodil, Dora, Dennis
and Danny don't know what to expect,
but their classmate Peg does.
She wants to be boss!

Here comes a fierce crow with a big
beak – is this the end of Dennis? It was meant
to be a splendid day out from school, but
he's got himself lost in a field. Will Daffodil,
Dora and Danny find him in time?

Human Beanies are dangerous, especially
when they're blowing smoke. Now there's
a fire in Under Shed, and the flames are
spreading! Can Daffodil, Dora, Dennis
and Danny save their home?

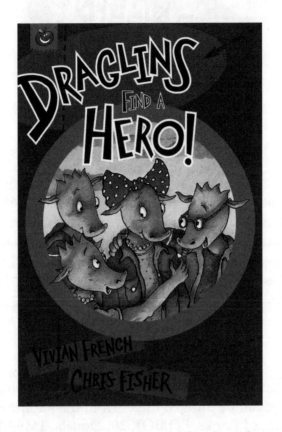

Summer holidays should be fun, but it
hasn't rained in weeks. There are cracks in the
Underground, and Daffodil, Dora, Dennis
and Danny's world is in terrible
danger – what can they do?

by Vivian French
illustrated by Chris Fisher

All priced at £8.99.

Draglins books are available from all good bookshops,
or can be ordered direct from the publisher:
Orchard Books, PO BOX 29, Douglas IM99 1BQ.
Credit card orders please telephone 01624 836000
or fax 01624 837033 or visit our website:
www.orchardbooks.co.uk
or e-mail: bookshop@enterprise.net for details.

To order please quote title, author and ISBN
and your full name and address.
Cheques and postal orders should be made
payable to 'Bookpost plc.'

Postage and packing is FREE within the UK
(overseas customers should add £2.00 per book).

Prices and availability are subject to change.